🌑 A GOLDEN BOOK · NEW YORK

NAUGHTY
BUNNY

Written and illustrated by
Richard Scarry

The little bunny didn't mean to be naughty.
But he didn't try very hard to be good.
He bothered his father at breakfast.
He spilled his cereal.

One day, the bunny's daddy said, "If you will try to be a good little bunny, I will bring you home a present from the city."

The little bunny promised to try.

"Goodbye, Daddy."

Mrs. Bunny turned on the television to the
little bunny's favorite program.

The little bunny turned the sound way up loud
and nearly frightened his mother out of her wits.

Oh, naughty bunny.

Mrs. Bunny gave him some crayons and a
coloring book. Look what he did.

Oh, naughty bunny.

The naughty bunny was sent to his room.

Poor little bunny.

Soon Mrs. Bunny looked in to see if he was being good.

What a mess the bunny made of his room! His dear sweet mother was exasperated.

She sent the bunny outside to play.

William, who was the bunny's best friend,
came over to play.

They leaped,
and they ran.

They kicked.

The little bunny
picked some flowers.

William ran quick to tell
the little bunny's mother.

At first Mrs. Bunny was furious.
But she just couldn't scold the little bunny.
Because he had picked them for her.

The little bunny pushed William for being a tattletale.

William fell into a mud puddle. Kersplash!

William went home crying.

William's mother telephoned the little
bunny's mother.

Oh, why couldn't her little bunny be a
nice little bunny like William?

Mrs. Bunny had to call the little bunny
twelve times to come to lunch.
He finally came.

He didn't want an egg sandwich.
He wanted peanut butter.
He wouldn't finish his milk.
He ate only half of his sandwich.

He made a fuss at naptime.
Oh, naughty bunny.

The little bunny didn't nap . . .

. . . until he heard his mother coming.

"Oh, what a dear, darling
bunny he is when he's asleep,"
she thought.

After the little bunny's nap, his mother sent him out to play.

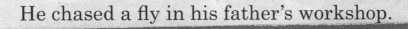

He chased a fly in his father's workshop.

He visited the chickens in the barnyard.
And left the gate open behind him.
Oh, naughty bunny.

When his father came home he asked, "Has he been a good little bunny?"

His mother answered, "Well, he tried to be a good little bunny, but sometimes he forgot."

Daddy gave the little bunny a present for trying to be good.

They sat down to supper.

The little bunny kissed his mother goodnight and his daddy gave him a piggyback ride to bed.

Instead of going right to sleep, the little bunny wanted a glass of water.

He wanted to go to the bathroom.

His mother went into his room to make him
go to sleep.

She told him that it made her very sad when
he was naughty.

The little bunny loved his mother dearly and
didn't like to see her sad.

He told her that tomorrow he was definitely
going to be a good little bunny.

And the next day the little bunny tried very hard to be good.

He didn't bother Daddy at breakfast.

He didn't spill his cereal.

He ate all his lunch.

He had his nap without a fuss.

He played nicely with William.

He was so good his mother didn't have to send him to his room, not once.

It was such fun to be good.

And then, after supper . . .

I LOVE MOMMY

The little bunny painted a picture
of himself.

It was a present for his mother.

His mother was very pleased.

She hugged him and kissed him
and she tucked him into bed.

And she said, "Oh, how I love my
naughty little angel."

BUNNIES

Written and illustrated by
Richard Scarry
Formerly titled *The Bunny Book*

The cottontail rabbit
has a little white tail.

Bunnies love to eat the cabbage . . .

. . . in Farmer Brown's garden.

Some rabbits have GIANT ears . . .

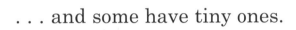

. . . and some have tiny ones.

The snowshoe
rabbit changes
the color of his
coat to white in
the winter . . .

. . . and to brown in the summer.

Rabbits can run very fast.

Angora rabbits have soft, cuddly fur.

Lop-eared rabbits have long, floppy ears.

There are many different kinds of rabbits.

DUTCH

VIENNA BLUE

FLEMISH GIANT

CHINCHILLA

COTTONTAIL

Rabbits have large families.

Rabbits like to
get all dressed up if
they are going to be
in a storybook.

At Easter time there are chocolate rabbits.

Turtles like to think they can beat rabbits
in a race . . .

. . . but they can't!

The BUNNY BOOK

By Patsy Scarry

Illustrated by
Richard Scarry

The daddy bunny tossed his baby in the air.
"What will our baby be when he grows up?"
asked the daddy bunny.

"He will be a policeman with gold buttons on his suit," said the mother bunny. "He will help little lost children find their mothers and daddies."

"Maybe he will be a circus clown," said the daddy bunny. "He will wear a funny suit and do funny tricks to make the children laugh."

"Why can't our baby be a cowboy?" asked the bunny brother. "If he grows up to be a cowboy he can ride horses at the rodeo."

But the baby bunny did not want to be a policeman
or a circus clown or a cowboy when he grew up.

He sat in his basket and smiled at his bunny family.
He knew what he would be.

"I think our baby bunny should be an airplane pilot," said the little bunny sister. "He could fly into the sky. And when he felt like having fun he could jump out in his parachute."

"Maybe he will be a fireman," said his Great-Aunt Bunny. "Then he could drive a big ladder truck to all the fires. He would be a brave fireman."

Great-Uncle Bunny wanted the baby to be an engineer on a big train.

"He would ring the bell when he was ready to start the train. And blow his horn, Toot! Toot! in the tunnels," said Great-Uncle Bunny.

But the baby bunny did not want to be an airplane pilot or a fireman or an engineer on a big train when he grew up. He nibbled on his carrot and looked wise. He knew what he wanted to be.

Old Grandaddy Bunny said:
"Just look at that baby. Why, any bunny can
see he is going to be a lion tamer!"

But Grandma Bunny said:
"I think he will be a nice little mailman who will bring a letter to every house and make the neighbors happy."

A hungry little bunny cousin wished that the
baby would have a candy store.

"He could make lollypops with funny faces
and give them to all the good children," wished
the hungry little bunny cousin.

But the baby bunny did not want to be a lion
tamer or a mailman or have a candy store.
He shook his rattle and smiled.
He would be what he wanted to be.

The little girl cousin said:
"It would be nice if our baby was a doctor.
Then he could put big bandages on little bumps."

"Oh dear no," said Aunt Bunny. "I am sure
he will be a lifeguard at the beach. He will save
people who can't swim."

"Not at all, my dear," said Uncle Bunny. "This little baby may grow up to be a farmer with a fine red tractor."

But the baby bunny did not want to be a doctor
or a lifeguard or a farmer with a fine red tractor
when he grew up.

He bounced on his daddy's knee and laughed.
Can you guess what he will be?

The baby bunny will be a daddy rabbit!
This is what he will be—with lots of little
bunny children to feed when they are hungry.

He will be a nice daddy who will chase the children when they want to be chased.

And give them presents on their birthdays.

He will read them a story when they are sleepy.

And tuck them into bed at night.
And that is what the baby bunny will grow up to be.
A daddy rabbit.